Germans
COMING TO AMERICA
A Bilingual Book

Deutsche WANDERN NACH AMERIKA AUS

beau·
designs

Story by Suzanne Simon Dietz
Illustrated by Lucy Vine
Translated by Anika Fetzner

Illustrated by: Lucy Vine

Translated by: Anika Fetzner

Layout and design by: BeauDesigns

ISBN: 978-0-9968870-6-9

First Edition

Published by:

beau designs

PO Box 496 • Youngstown, NY 14174
www.BeauDesigns.biz

Dedication
In memory of all our ancestors who came
to America from Germany
especially Anna Barbara Holder and Johann Friedrich Diez.

Widmung
In Gedenken an all unsere Vorfahren die
von Deutschland nach Amerika kamen
besonders Anna Barbara Holder und Johann Friedrich Diez.

Anna Barbara
26 September 1846 – 11 June 1927

Friedrich
4 April 1843 – 11 November 1927

Author's Note

In 1811 the West Battery, also known as the Southwest Battery, was built to defend New York City from the British during the War of 1812, but never saw action. Several years later the Fort was renamed Castle Clinton and in 1821 began its history as "Castle Garden" and used for a number of public purposes.

The Fort's distinction resulted from its history as the landing depot for immigrants. In the 1970s Castle Garden became part of the National Park Service in Battery Park on the southern tip of Manhattan and resumed the name Castle Clinton.

From 1855 – 1890 about eight million people entered the United States at Castle Garden. The largest numbers of immigrants came from Germany and Ireland for political and/or economic reasons.

In 1886 the French gift of the Statue of Liberty greeted the arriving immigrants and six years later Ellis Island became the Federal Processing Center. Ellis Island officially opened on January 1, 1892, and processed millions of people particularly Russian Jews and Italians.

This historical narrative of Johnnie's Adventures is based on the true story of one of the many German families that came to America. Enjoy!

~Suzanne Simon Dietz

Zusatz der Autorin

In 1811 wurde die West Battery, sie wurde auch als southwest Battery bezeichnet, gegründet um New York City von den Briten während des Krieges von 1812 zu verteidigen, jedoch wurde sie nie eingesetzt. Mehrere Jahre später wurde das Fort zu Castle Clinton umbenannt und in 1821 begann es seine Geschichte als "Castle Garden" (Schlossgarten) und wurde für verschiedene öffentliche Gelegenheiten benutzt.

Das Fort wurde durch seine Historie als Auffanglager fur Immigranten benutzt. In den 1970zigern wurde der Castle Garden dem National Park Dienst in Battery Park, dem am südlichsten Teil von Manhatten, zugeteilt und wurde von da an wieder Castle Clinton genannt.

Zwischen 1855-1890 kamen ca. acht Millionen Menschen in die Vereinigten Staaten durch Castle Garden. Der grösste Teil der Einwanderer kam aus Deutschland und Irland aus politischen oder wirtschaftlichen Gründen.

Ab 1886 begrüsste das französische Geschenk die Freiheitsstatue die ankommenden Immigranten und sechs Jahre später wurde Ellis Island zum staatlichen Abwicklungszentrum. Ellis Island wurde offiziel am 1. Januar 1892 eröffnet und wickelte Millionen Menschen hauptsächlich russische Juden und Italiener ab.

Diese historische Erzählung von Johnnies Abendteuer beruht auf einer wahren Begebenheit einer der vielen Deutschen Familien die nach Amerika kamen. Viel Spass!

~Suzanne Simon Dietz

Left:

Castle Clinton, September 1998

Photo by author
Foto vom Autor

Johnnie's Adventures / Johnnie's Abenteuer

The New Colossus

Not like the brazen giant of Greek fame,
With conquering limbs astride from land to land;
Here at our sea – washed, sunset gates shall stand
A mighty woman with a torch, whose flame
Is the imprisoned lightning, and her name
Mother of Exiles. From her beacon – hand
Glows world-wide welcome; her mild eyes command
The air – bridged harbor that twin cities frame.
"Keep, ancient lands, your storied pomp!" cries she
With silent lips. "Give me your tired, your poor,
Your huddled masses yearning to breathe free,
The wretched refuse of your teeming shore.
Send these, the homeless, tempest – tossed to me,
I lift my lamp beside the golden door!"

~ Emma Lazarus

*The sonnet by American poet Lazarus written
in 1883 was engraved on a plaque inside
Lady Liberty's pedestal in 1903.*

Der Neue Koloss

Nicht wie der freche Gigant aus
griechischem Ruhm,
Mit erobernden Gliedern ausgestreckt
von Land zu Land;
Hier an unserem Meer – gewaschen, Sonnenuntergangs Tore sollen stehen
Eine mächtige Frau mit Fackel, dessen Flamme
Ist der eingefangene Blitz, und ihr Name
Mutter der Ausgestossenen. Von ihrem Lichtstrahl – Hand
Glimmert Weltweites Wilkommen; Ihre freundlichen Augen fordern
Die Luft – überbrückend Hafen
der berühmten Zwillingsstadt.
"Behaltet, alten Landes,
eure Geschichten Pracht!" weint sie
Mit stummen Lippen. "Gebt mir
Eure Müden, Eure Armen,
Eure zusammengedrängten Massen die
sich nach freien Atem sehnen,
Den erbärmlichen Abfall der an euren
Küsten wimmelt.
Schickt mir diese, die Obdachlosen, stürmisch – mir entgegen geworfen,
Ich hebe mcine Laterne neben den
goldenen Toren!"
~ *Emma Lazarus*

*Das Sonett wurde von amerikanischem Dichter Lazarus
in 1883 geschrieben und auf die Plakette am Sockel der
Freiheitsstatue in 1903 eingraviert.*

Johnnie's Adventures / *Johnnie's Abenteuer*

The Statue of Liberty was dedicated in 1886.

Die Freiheitsstatue wurde in 1886 gewidment.

Bottle warmer brought to America by Friedrich and Anna Barbara.

Der Flaschenwärmer wurde von Friedrich und Anna Barbara nach Amerika gebracht.

Anna Barbara's devotional book.

Anna Barbara's Gebetsbuch (in Altdeutsch).

It had been a busy day on the farm. All day long Johnnie climbed up and down the ladder picking apples. His pet pig Guinevere played in the dirt. Guinevere followed Johnnie everywhere.

But now, the sun began to set over the lake. Johnnie dragged the ladder towards the barn.

Es war ein ereignisreicher Tag auf dem Bauernhof gewesen. Den ganzen Tag stieg Johnnie die Leiter auf und ab und pflückte Äpfel. Sein Lieblingsschwein Guinevere spielte im Dreck. Guinevere folgte Johnnie überall hin.

Jedoch jetzt began die Sonne über dem See unter zu gehen. Johnnie zerrte die Leiter in Richtung Scheune.

Johnnie ran into the house with Guinevere right behind. "Please, please Mama, tell me the story tonight."

"What story?" His mother smiled. Guinevere's ears perked up.

"Mama, you know which story," Johnnie said. Guinevere nodded.

"I will tell you after dinner. But first get washed up," his mother said.

Johnnie rannte in Haus mit Guinevere direkt hinter sich. "Bitte, bitte, Mama, erzähl mir eine Geschichte heute Abend."

"Welche Geschichte?" lächelte seine Mutter. Guinevers Ohren spitzten sich.

"Mama, du weisst doch welche Geschichte," sagte Johnnie. Guinevere nickte

"Ich erzähle sie dir nach dem Abendbrot. Aber jetzt geh dich erst einmal waschen," sagte seine Mutter.

Germans Coming to America / Deutsche wandern nach Amerika aus

That evening Johnnie played with Guinevere, while his mother read her prayer book.

The chair stopped rocking. His mother began in a quiet voice. "We left Germany to come to America. We are immigrants."

"What is an immigrant?" Johnnie asked.

"An immigrant is someone who leaves their home and moves to another country."

An diesem Abend spielte Johnnie mit Guinevere während dessen seine Mutter ihr Gebetbuch las.

Der Stuhl hörte auf zu schaukeln. Seine Mutter begann mit einer sanften Stimme. "Wir verliessen Deutschland um nach Amerika zu kommen. Wir sind Einwanderer."

"Was ist ein Einwanderer?" fragte Johnnie.

"Ein Einwanderer ist jemand der seine Heimat verlässt und in ein anderes Land zieht."

His mother took a deep breath and sighed. "We lived in a little village very, very far away."

"Why did you and Papa leave your home?" Johnnie asked.

"Your father wanted his own farm. His older brother worked the family farm in Germany. Other relatives lived in America."

Johnnie smiled. He liked doing chores and chasing Guinevere around the oak tree on their farm.

Seine Mutter holte tief Luft und seufste. "Wir lebten in einem kleinen Dorf sehr, sehr weit weg von hier."

"Warum hast du und Papa euer zu Hause verlassen?" fragte Johnnie.

"Dein Vater wollte seinen eigenen Bauernhof. Sein älterer Bruder bewirtschaftete den Familienhof in Deutschland. Andere Verwandte wohnten schon in Amerika."

Johnnie grinste. Er mochte es seine Aufgaben zu erledigen und Guinevere um den Eichenbaum auf ihrem Bauernhof zu jagen.

Johnnie's father saved money for many months to pay for the trip to America.

"We had to decide what to bring," his mother said. "We packed our trunk with clothes, some of your father's tools, and my prayer book."

"What about me? What did you bring for me?" Johnnie asked.

His mother pointed to the baby bottle warmer. Sometimes the family used it to warm their beds.

Johnnie's Vater sparte sein Geld für viele Monate um die Reise nach Amerika zu bezahlen.

"Wir mussten uns entscheiden was wir bringen konnten,"sagte seine Mutter. "Wir packten unsere Truhe mit Kleidern, einigen Werkzeugen deines Vaters, und mein Gebetbuch."

"Was war mit mir? Was habt ihr mir mitgenommen?" fragte Johnnie.

Seine Mutter zeigte auf den Baby Flaschenwärmer. Manchmal benutzte die Familie diesen um ihre Betten an zu wärmen.

"What was it like to leave home?" Johnnie asked his mother.

"Our family and neighbors came to say goodbye. We left after Christmas."

A few tears ran down his mother's cheeks. Johnnie and Guinevere moved closer to his mother.

"First, we travelled a long way on a wagon."

"Wie war es euer zu Hause zu verlassen?" fragte Johnnie seine Mutter.

"Unsere Familie und Nachbarn kamen um sich zu verabschieden. Wir sind nach Weihnachten gegangen"

Ein paar Tränen rollten seiner Mutter die Wangen herunter. Johnnie und Guinevere rutschten dichter an seine Mutter heran.

"Zuerst reisten wir eine lange Strecke mit einer Kutsche."

Germans Coming to America / Deutsche wandern nach Amerika aus

"At the sea, we boarded a sailing schooner with a smoke stack. The boat rocked up and down across the ocean. Sometimes the waves rolled over the deck."

Guinevere squirmed. She had never been on a boat before.

"Mother how long did it take to get to America? Was it fun? Was it a big boat?"

"The boat was crowded. The men talked about farming."

"An der Küste angekommen, gingen wir an Bord eines grossen Schiffes mit einem Schornstein. Das Schiff schaukelte hoch und runter über den Ozean. Manchmal rollten die Wellen über das Deck."

Guinevere kauerte sich hin. Sie war noch nie auf einem Schiff.

"Mutter wie lang dauerte es bis nach Amerika zu kommen? Hat es Spass gemacht? War es ein grosses Schiff?"

"Das Schiff war sehr voll. Die Männer sprachen über die Landwirtschaft."

Days and weeks passed. Some people got sick.

"It took six weeks before we saw America's shore." Guinevere and Johnnie's eyes opened wide.

"We arrived at the government station called Castle Garden."

The inspector asked, "Where are you going? Do you have any money? Do you have any relatives in America? Is anyone in your family sick?"

Tage und Wochen vergingen. Manche Menschen wurden krank.

"Es dauerte sechs Wochen bevor wir die Amerikanische Küste sahen." Guinevere und Johnnie's Augen wurden ganz gross.

"Wir kamen an der staatlichen Auffangstelle 'Castle Garden' an."

Der Inspektor fragte, "Wohin gehen sie? Haben sie Geld? Haben sie Verwandte in Amerika? Ist irgend jemand in ihrer Familie krank?"

Johnnie's Adventures / Johnnie's Abenteuer

Germans Coming to America / Deutsche wandern nach Amerika aus

After the family went through inspection, they made their way to the railroad station. People and wagons filled the noisy streets of New York City.

"After several hours, we boarded the train to leave the city. We looked and looked out the window at our new country."

Johnnie and Guinevere yawned. "Are we there yet?"

Nachdem die Familie durch die Inspektion gegangen war, gingen sie in Richtung Bahnstation. Menschen und Kutschen füllten die lauten Strassen von New York City.

"Nach einigen Stunden, stiegen wir in den Zug und verliessen die Stadt. Wir schauten und schauten aus dem Fenster uns sahen uns unser neues Land an."

Johnnie und Guinevere gähnten. "Sind wir endlich da?"

"The train rattled on the tracks all day. We reached our station stop in the midst of a snowstorm."

Johnnie and Guinevere shivered.

"Your uncle met us in a sleigh. The horse struggled through the snow. It took us all afternoon to get home. We were very tired."

"Der Zug ratterte den ganzen Tag über die Gleise. Wir kamen an unserer Haltestelle in mitten eines Schneesturmes an."

Johnnie und Guinevere zitterten.

"Dein Onkel holte uns mit einem Schlitten ab. Das Pferd kämpfte sich durch den Schnee. Es dauerte den ganzen Nachmittag bis wir es nach Hause schafften. Wir waren sehr müde."

Germans Coming to America / Deutsche wandern nach Amerika aus

"Finally we reached our new home," his mother said.
Johnnie and Guinevere jumped up. "Hooray, we made it," he shouted.
Now Johnnie's family had their own farm.
His mother smiled and rose from the chair.
"God bless America and our new home!"
The end.

"Endlich erreichten wir unser neues zu Hause, " sagte seine Mutter.
Johnnie und Guinevere sprangen hoch. "Hurah, wir haben es geschafft," schrie er.
Nun hatten Johnnie's Familie ihren eigenen Bauernhof.
Seine Mutter lächelte und erhebte sich vom Stuhl.
"Gott segne Amerika und unser neues Heim!"
Ende.

For the Adult Reader

Johnnie's uncle, Johannes (John) Diez, came to America in 1853 and settled in Newfane, Niagara County, New York, before purchasing a 167-acre farm on the Youngstown-Wilson Road. He built one of the first brick homes in Wilson for more than $6,000 in 1857. Cousins Christian Friedrich, Jakob, and Wilhelm Diez settled around Newstead, Royalton, Clarence and Lockport, New York. The families emigrated from Dettingen unter Teck, southeast of Stuttgart, Germany.

In the mid-19th century, crop failures in Germany, the Irish Potato Famine, and political discontent led to a period of significant immigration to America. In 1850 the United States Census surveyed "nativity" for the first time. The Homestead Act of 1862 offered free land in the west up to 160 acres spurring an influx of immigrants.

Johann Friedrich and Anna Barbara Diez and their newborn son sailed to America in 1867 on the SS *Union*, a 325-foot long ship with two masts and a steam funnel.

Anna Maria "Mary" Diez Lloyd described her father Friedrich as an energetic, ambitious, and highly respected man. He bought five farms in the Town of Porter, which he eventually transferred to his five sons. Friedrich was proud to be an American citizen and quickly became fluent in English and requested that it be spoken in his home. He was the sole Trustee of Rural School No. 8 at the crossroads of Youngstown-Wilson and Clapsaddle (now Braley Road) in the Town of Porter.

Friedrich's homestead farm on Lake Ontario was taken by eminent domain for the creation of Four Mile State Park. Park officials consider the farm's red oak tree as possibly the oldest in New York State.

Raymond Dietz, a great-grandson, lives on one of the five farms purchased in 1886 for $2,500. In 1913 Friedrich sold this farm to his son John F. Diez for $2,000.00 and as a part of the consideration "the second party hereto is to furnish ten bushels of potatoes, one barrel of apples and three bushels of peaches each year for and during the period of the natural life of party of first part or wife. Said produce to be delivered at the residence of said first party on request."

Many of Friedrich's descendants still live in the town.

Für den Erwachsenen Leser

Johnnie's Onkel, Johannes (John) Diez, kam 1853 nach Amerika und liess sich in Newfane, Niagara County, New York, nieder bevor er den 67.5 Hektar großen Bauernhof an der Youngstown-Wilson Road kaufte. Er baute eines der ersten Steinhäuser in Wilson für mehr als $6.000 in 1857. Die Cousins Christian Friedrich, Jakob und Wilhelm Diez liessen sich um Newstead, Royalton, Clarence und Lockport, New York nieder. Die Familien wanderten von Dettingen unter Teck südlich von Stuttgart Deutschland ein.

Mitte des 19ten Jahrhunderts führten Ernteausfälle in Deutschland, die Irische Kartoffel Hungersnot, und politische Unruhen zu einer starken Einwanderungswelle nach Amerika. In 1850 hielt der United States Census die erste Volkszählung mit Abstammung. Der Homestead Act von 1862 bot freies Land im Westen bis zu 160 Acre (64.7 Hektar) was zu einem Einwanderungs Wachstum führte.

Johann Friedrich, Anna Barbara Diez und ihr neugeborener Sohn segelten in 1867 auf der SS Union, einem 325 Fuss(99m) langen Schiff mit zwei Masten und einem Dampf Schornstein, nach Amerika.

Anna Maria "Mary" Diez Lloyd beschrieb ihren Vater Friedrich als einen sehr energischen, ehrgeizigen, und sehr respektierten Mann. Er kaufte fünf Bauernhöfe in der Stadt Porter, welche er schliesslich auf seine fünf Söhne überschrieb. Friedrich war sehr stolz Amerikaner zu sein und lernte es schnell Englisch fliessend zu sprechen und er bestand darauf das es in seinem Haus gesprochen wurde. Er war der einzige Treuhänder der ländlichen Schule Nr. 8 die an der Kreuzung Youngstown-Wilson und Clapsaddle (jetzt Braley Road) in der Stadt Porter gelegen war.

Friedrich's heimstättischer Bauernhof am Ontario See wurde vom Staat mit Eminenter Domäne eingezogen bei der Einrichtung des Four Mile State Parks. Die Parkbeamten vermuten das die Roteiche des Bauernhofes wahrscheinlich der älteste von New York State sei.

Raymond Dietz, ein Urenkel, lebt noch auf einem der fünf Bauernhöfen die in 1886 für $2500 gekauft wurden. 1913 verkaufte Friedrich diesen Bauernhof an seinen Sohn John F. Diez für $2000 als Teil eines Vertrages "hiermit stimmt die zweite Partei zu zehn Büschel Kartoffeln, ein Fass Äpfel, und drei Büschel Pfirsiche jedes Jahr und für die Lebenszeit der ersten Partei sowie dessen Ehefrau anzuliefern. Dieser Ertrag soll an die Residenz der ersten Partei auf Bestellung geliefert werden."

Viele Nachkommen von Friedrich leben heute noch in der Stadt.

Photo of Friedrich & Anna Barbara in later years.

Foto von Friedrich und Anna Barbara in ihren späteren Jahren.

Time Period	Numbers of Immigrants Arriving in the US
	Zeiträume in denen Einwanderer in den Vereinigten Staaten ankamen
1821 – 1830	143,439
1831 – 1840	599,125
1841 – 1850	1,713,251
1851 – 1860	2,598,214
1861 – 1970	2,314,825
1871 – 1880	2,812,191
1881 – 1890	5,246,613
1891 – 1890	5,246,613
1881 – 1885	1 million Germans arrive; peak of German immigration 1 Millionen Deutsche wanderten ein; Hoch der Deutschen Einwanderung
1881 – 1920	2 million European Jews arrive 2 Millionen Europäische Juden wanderten ein

Source: Harvard University Open Collections Program, Aspiration, Acculturation and Impact Immigration to the United States, 1789 – 1930.

Quelle: Harvard University Open Collections Program, Aspiration, Acculturation and Impact Immigration to the United States, 1789 – 1930.

About the Author, Illustrator, Translator and Publisher

Suzanne Simon Dietz — Author

Author and historian Suzanne Simon Dietz's publications document local and World War II era history. Her publication *My True Course*, the biography of Dutch Van Kirk (navigator of the Enola Gay), received the 2013 Silver Medal by the Military Writers Society of America.

Lucy Vine — Illustrator

Lucy, high school junior, illustrator, and artist is excited to have worked on her first collaborative project. She looks forward to furthering her education and pursuing a career in the visual arts.

Anika Fetzner — Translator

Anika is an immigrant herself, who met her husband during her exchange year in the United States. She is a homemaker and mother to four lively children. It is also her first collaboration on a book, which challenged her but also was a lot of fun.

Amy Freiermuth — Publisher

Amy, owner of BeauDesigns — Graphic Design and Printing, is excited to publish her third children's story, and is especially happy to see Guinevere has returned. Johnnie has taught her a bit about local history while having fun on his adventures. She hopes that you feel the same!

Ueber die Autorin, Illustratorin, Übersetzerin, und Herausgeberin

Suzanne Simon Dietz — Autorin
Autorin und Historikerin Susanne Simon Dietz Veröffentlichungen dokumentieren lokale Geschichte sowie den Zeitraum des Zweiten Weltkrieges. Sie veröffentlichte "My True Course" die Biographie von Dutch Van Kirk (Navigator der Enola Gay), wofür sie die Silbermedaille der Military Writers Society of America in 2013 erhielt.

Lucy Vine — Illustratorin
Lucy, ist ein High School Junior (11.Klasse), und eine Künstlerin die sehr glücklich darüber war an diesem ersten Gemeinschaftsprojekt gearbeitet zu haben. Sie ist interessiert daran ihre Schule abzuschliessen und danach eine Karriere in Visueller Kunst anzustreben.

Anika Fetzner — Uebersetzerin
Anika ist selbst eine Einwanderin die während ihres Austauschjahres in den Vereinigten Staaten ihren Ehemann kennengelernt hat. Sie ist Hausfrau und Mutter von vier aufgeweckten Kindern. Für sie ist es ebenfalls ihr erstes Gemeinschaftsprojekt, was sie herausgefordert aber auch viel Spass bereitet hat.

Amy Freiermuth — Herausgeberin
Amy, Besitzer des BeauDesign — Graphic Design and Printing, ist freudig ihr drittes Kinderbuch herauszubringen, und sehr erfreut das Guinevere wieder zurückgekommen ist. Johnnie hat ihr sehr viel über die Lokale Geschichte beigebracht während dessen er seine Abenteuer erlebt. Sie hofft das sie es ebenso empfinden!